T0144955

Three Little Blackbirds walking on the Lawn

JENNIE DUNCAN

To order additional copies of this book, contact:
Xlibris LLC
1-888-795-4274
www.Xlibris.com
Orders@Xlibris.com

To Robert, Melania, D'Andre, and their parents for your support

Special thanks to Joyce Warner, Elisient Maeve Vernon, and Gillian Francis for editing suggestions   −J.R.D.

One cool and cloudy morning, three little blackbirds landed on a freshly cut lawn in front of a house.

Their names were Barky, Darky and Larky. They had flown all the way from the north to the south to escape the dread of the cold winter months.

The little blackbirds had traveled for days, stopping only at sunset for food and rest. Happy to have arrived in warm climate, they went in search of food.

They hopped here and there in the grass searching for worms and bugs.

Soon they came to a small shopping mall.

Barky, Darky, and Larky flew into a tree across from a large food store. They watched from a distance as some other blackbirds flew from nearby trees to the ground and then back into the trees. They were picking up something yellow from the ground. Grains! There were heaps and heaps of yellow grains on the ground.

"Chirpy, Chirpy, Chirp, Chirp! Food at last," chirped Darky as he flew head-on into a heap of grains. The others followed and dove into the grains.

The little blackbirds ate and ate and ate, moving from one heap of tiny, yellow grains to another. They did not even care about the people who walked close by going into and out of the stores.

Larky was so busy pecking through the grains that he did not see a car approaching. The driver slowed. He had seen all the birds busy pecking at the grains. Then, Larky saw the car and, frightened, he flew up into the air at such speed that he startled the other birds. They all flew in various directions into different treetops, chirping in fear.

Poor Larky! He just barely missed being hit. He sighed deeply and said, "Oops! That was close. I think we'd better get away from here." He quickly flew away. Barky and Darky flew after him even though they wanted to stay and eat more grains.

Patches of dark clouds soon covered the sky. The blackbirds knew that the rains would come soon. They were familiar with the weather changes, having traveled for such a long time. But they continued flying south.

The three little blackbirds came to a neighborhood with lovely homes and beautiful gardens and lawns. The houses were built so closely to each other that the roofs seemed to touch each other. Barky, Darky, and Larky liked these houses better than those in the North, which were so tall that they seemed to touch the sky.

The three little blackbirds felt happy and free as they flew from tree to tree in this beautiful neighborhood.

From a tree, Darky looked down and saw two white ducks. They were waddling slowly beside each other. They were on a lawn. Their broad tails swished from side to side. The movement of their tails caused their bodies to sway as though they were moving to a slow dance rhythm. The ducks were searching for bugs, snails, and worms. When they found one, they raised their heads and swung from side to side with the food in their beaks. Fascinated, the birds watched the ducks. Then suddenly Darky cried out excitedly.

"Look!" he said, pointing his beak towards the ground. "Aren't those our big cousins from our grandfather's family?"

Barky chirped, excited as well, "Yes, let's go down and see what they found. Maybe we, too, can find some!"

"Chirpy! Chirpy! Chirp! Chirp!" Darky and Larky chimed in agreement, and then they flew down onto the green lawn. The ducks did not seem bothered by the blackbirds. They continued to scratch among the roots of the grass.

Barky, Darky, and Larky joined the ducks in search of worms and bugs but they did not find any in the grass.

Larky decided to fly away, but just then, there was a sudden flash of lightning, and then a loud clash of thunder. Larky flew up in the air but came down quickly when the lightning flashed again. Although he was a little frightened, he stayed with Barky and Darky on the lawn. Barky and Darky joked softly about Larky being such a coward.

Barky, Darky, and Larky did not find any worms or bugs on that lawn. They flew onto a nearby metal-link fence and began to prune their feathers.

After a while, the birds decided to continue on their journey south. Just as they were about to fly away, Larky spotted a large log floating on the lake a few feet away. A dark-brown turtle sat on the log, which the gentle waves were pushing upstream.

"Hello, my friend! What a lovely day to be swimming upstream!" Larky exclaimed, as the turtle sailed by.

"You bet it is", the turtle chuckled and held its short, tiny head high enough to greet them. "Why don't you join me? You will see some of the most beautiful scenery. You will also find many fish to catch."

Barky, Darky, and Larky needed no further prompting. Up and away they went, landing softly behind the turtle on the log. As the log moved upstream, the turtle pointed out the neighborhood homes they were passing.

The group of one turtle and three blackbirds came to a house at the edge of the lake. There was concrete wall separating the house from the lake. More than a dozen white birds sat on the wall. They were pruning their feathers with their long pointed beaks.

As the blackbirds and the turtle passed by, the turtle greeted the white birds, "Good morning, White Birds! How do you do? Please meet my friends."

"Hello, dear Turtle!" The white birds answered in a chorus. "We're glad to see you and your friends."

The white birds flew from the wall in a flock and circled the log a couple of times. Then they flew onto the log, landing one beside the other. They encircled the turtle and the three blackbirds. It was a beautiful sight!

Barky, Darky, and Larky noticed that the white birds had lanky pink legs which held their pretty white bodies upright. Their beaks were long with a narrow bend at the tips. Patches of large brown feathers nestled beneath their wings. These white birds were beautiful birds. Immediately, the blackbirds sensed a strong bond between themselves and the white birds.

The turtle, the blackbirds and the white birds traveled together upstream on the log for a few minutes. Then, Barky looked down into the water. Fish of all sizes were swimming gracefully below the log.

"Look! Fish!" He called out and flew off the log towards the water. "Let's go fishing!"

The birds flew off the log and dove into the water. Barky was the first to pick up a fish. He darted downstream towards the flat concrete wall intending to perch there to have his meal. Two of the white birds followed him. Not wanting to lose his fish, Barky raced on. Darky, Larky and the white birds were right behind him. Some had a couple of small fish in their beaks. They were going full speed, but cautiously, downstream holding the fishes in their beaks. Before they knew it, the meal time had turned into a bird race.

Flap! Flap! Flap! Flap! their wings echoed as they sped downstream.

Barky led the flock of birds for a while and then he made a slight swerve and flew upstream. The other birds were in hot pursuit. He managed to swallow his fish while in flight, and so he was free to compete. He felt so excited!

He chirped as loudly as he could. The white birds joined in as they fluttered upstream again.

"CHI, CHI, CHIP, CHIP!

CHI, CHI, CHIP! CHIP!

CHI, CHI, CHIP! CHIP!"

By this time, the turtle had swum quietly downstream to catch up with his friends. He got as far as the wall and sat on it so he could watch the race. As the birds winged by, the turtle cheered, and cheered, and cheered. He lifted his body as high as he could and... SPLASH! He lost his balance, and fell into the lake.

Poor turtle! How he wished he could fly!

Turtle crawled clumsily back onto the wall, and was just in time to see the birds gliding downstream. The birds flew onto the wire fence nearby and settled beside each other. Some stood on one leg as they tried to catch their breath. The white birds looked like large cotton patches neatly lined along the fence.

"Chirp! Chirp! Chirp!" They sang happily.

A lively, healthy spaniel suddenly appeared. It rushed at the birds, barking excitedly. All the birds flew away in a flurry. They flew rapidly upstream to get away from the spaniel.

Barky, Darky, and Larky flew with the white birds for a short distant and then bid them goodbye.

"Goodbye, my friends! We enjoyed your company", said Larky.

"We must be on our way. I hope we will meet again", added Darky.

The white birds flapped their wings heartily and wished them a good stay in the south. Then, they disappeared in the distance.

The three little blackbirds landed on a lawn close by. The sound of thunder warned them that the rains were coming. Large black clouds were hovering above. A flash of lightening came every now and then. Nevertheless, the three little blackbirds continued to walk on the lawn and peck at the grass.

Then, down came the rain! Heavy raindrops splashed on the thirsty grass. Barky, Darky, and Larky continued to walk on the lawn as raindrops bounced freely off their shiny, black feathers, leaving them damp and cool.

Barky hopped about on the grass chirping happily.

CHIRPY, CHIRPY, CHIRP, CHIRP!

CHIRPY, CHIRPY, CHIRP, CHIRP!

CHIRPY, CHIRPY, CHIRP CHIRP!

What a lovely feeling! Oh! I LOVE this rainy day!" He exclaimed. He hopped here and there on his long, skinny legs, pausing every now and then to comb through the damp feathers on his back, using his pointed beak. The raindrops felt so good that he wished they would last forever. His feathers were now glossy blue. They looked as if he had been oiled over and over again.

Darky and Larky were having the same experience. The water trickled down their wings and they flapped hard to get rid of it.

The three little blackbirds continued walking around on the lawn in the rain, chirping even louder and more excited than before.

"CHIRPY! CHIRPY! CHIRP! CHIRP!

Let it rain, let it rain,

Oh! How I love this rainy day!"

Darky and Larky flew up into a tree in front of a house. They sat one behind the other on a thin, dried branch that shook and tipped towards the ground. Barky saw when they flew off just in time before the branch broke away from the tree. He was so amused that he flew up and down, up and down, chirping excitedly.

"CHIRPY, CHIRPY, CHIRP CHIRP!

What a lovely feeling!

Oh! I LOVE this rainy day!"

Barky was so happy and excited that he lost his balance and landed head first on the balcony of the house, right on top of something black and furry.

"Woof! Woof! Woof! Woof!

"Woof! Woof! Woof! Woof!"

Barky was so frightened that he flew away as fast as his shiny wings could carry him. He didn't even look back for Darky and Larky. He flew straight across the lake and landed on a shrub. He could hardly breathe. He was shaking like a leaf.

Darky and Larky heard the commotion. They recognized the sound of the big dog. Afraid, they followed Barky straight across the lake.

The birds found a dry spot under a shed. They squeezed themselves together so they could fit in the small space. The rain fell and fell and fell. They were about to fall asleep, lulled by the rain, when they heard a squeaky sound.

"Shhhhh!" Darky whispered. "I have a sudden feeling that we won't be here for very long."

Creak! Creak! Crack! Crack!

That was the sound of a door opening.

"Oh no! Not again!", whispered Larky and flew out as fast as he could. Barky and Darky followed closely behind him. They flew into a tall mango tree near a house. From their position in the mango tree, they saw a beautiful woman and a little girl walk out of the house onto the balcony. The woman was holding a flowerpot in her hands.

"Look, Mommy!" said the little girl. "It's raining. This is just what our daisy needs."

The little girl was about six years old. She had long curly hair that was pulled back in a ponytail revealing her baby-like face. Her mother's hair was blonde and long, falling onto her shoulders. The birds watched as she bent to put down the flowerpot. Strands of hair fell forward onto her face. With one hand, she gently pushed the loose strands back in place. Then she carefully placed the pot with the daisy on a flat surface where the raindrops could reach it. She watched the raindrops for a while, and then they both went back into the house.

The heavy rains continued for a few hours. Then the sun came out and shone as bright as ever.

Barky, Darky and Larky shuffled in their spots in the tall mango tree. They felt a little tired and hungry. Their stomachs ached once more, but they weren't sure if it was safe to go back in search of worms and bugs.

"What do we do now?" Darky asked. "I am starving. Soon, I won't have enough energy to fly. I think I am going to risk it though. I am going down on the lawn again. Are you coming?"

After a moment of silence, Larky agreed that they should fly down on the lawn again.

Barky was not very happy with the idea but his stomach was really aching. He could feel the pain stretching like a long thread inside his body. He sighed deeply and flew down to join the others.

The little birds thrust their long, pointed beaks into the soil and searched here and there for worms. It was easier now because the rain had softened the soil.

Before long, Darky gave a loud chirp. He jumped up and down in excitement. He was pulling frantically at something very, very long. A worm at last!

The three blackbirds wrestled for the worm. Darky got it and with it in his beak, he flew up and perched in a tree nearby. Larky and Barky perched joyfully beside him. They ate the worm hungrily and then went back to search for more worms. This time, Barky chirped happily.

"CHIRPY, CHIRPY, CHIRP CHIRP!

 What a lovely feeling!

Food at last! Food at last!"

Darky decided to go back to the exact spot where he first found the worm. He pecked and pecked and pecked. Before long, he found another long worm, and then another, and another. Soon, they were having a worm feast.

As the birds were chirping happily, the beautiful woman was coming out of the house again. She was going to get the daisy. As she opened the door, she heard the chirping of the birds. It was the sweetest sound to her. She had not heard the sweet chirping of blackbirds in a long time. Her face lit up as she listened. As she was trying to identify where the sound was coming from, up flew Barky, Darky, and Larky in a nearby tree. They were chirping, chirping, chirping all the way to the top. The sound filled the pretty woman with joy.

"That's lovely! Won't you please come back?" She called after them. "Your chirping is music in my ears. I really love it. God sent you here today to cheer me up. *Pleeeease*, please come back!"

But Barky, Darky, and Larky were no longer visible as they shuffled in between the green leaves of the mango tree.

Looking slightly disappointed, the woman gently picked up her daisy. Hearing the chirping blackbirds made her feel very happy. It was a welcomed sound, which brought back fond memories of her childhood. Those were days when she would hear the blackbirds in the tall evergreen trees. It was always a pleasure to listen to their chirping.

Now, the pretty woman tried to imitate the chirping of the three blackbirds.

"Cheesy, Cheesy, Chip, Chip!" she sang as she merrily walked back into the house. Then she smiled in embarrassment at her effort.

In the evening, the rain came again, down, down, down, and covered the lawn with millions of tiny raindrops. Barky, Darky, and Larky cuddled between two large branches of the mango tree. They waited patiently for the rain to stop. They watched the water as it dropped from leaf to leaf all the way to the ground. It seemed like the rain would never stop.

Larky felt droplets of water trickling on his wings. The water felt so cold that he opened his wings and shuffled them quickly. The movement pushed Barky and Darky off balance. They flew out into the open space in search of another place.

"Come along", they called to Larky. "Let's go to the big oak tree down the street."

"Chirpy! Chirpy! Chirp! Chirp!" Off they went.

The raindrops were so cold and strong that the little blackbirds felt them like needle pricks against their now soaked bodies. Poor Barky, Darky, and Larky! How they wished they had stayed among the branches of the mango tree!

The sky was white as snow. The birds could hardly see anything ahead of them. Larky felt a little afraid but he flew on with Barky and Darky following close by.

Suddenly, Larky called out, "Look! Can you see those dark specks in the distance?"

"Yes, I see them, too. What do you think they are?" asked Darky.

"I think they are our friends from out of town. Isn't today the day for our big parade?" Larky shouted excitedly.

The blackbirds had been distracted these past hours. This made them forget that at this time of the year, flocks of blackbirds paraded on power lines in the day, from morning until late afternoon.

Larky's wings found extra energy as he flew as fast as he could towards the dark specks ahead. Sure enough, he saw many of his friends, all strung alongside each other on the power lines at the intersection of North Street and South Street. From behind, Barky and Darky could see them. They suddenly felt light-hearted and happy as they came near to the other birds.

Within a few minutes, the three little blackbirds landed beside four other birds that were enjoying the scene below. The evening traffic was building up at the stoplights. Barky, Darky, and Larky recognized these birds from the street parade last fall.

At the street parade, hundreds of blackbirds come from various locations. They playfully fly around or sit in neat rows on the power lines. This is a beautiful sight for human eyes, as the birds move from one place to another on the power line, and then magically fall back into neat rows.

"Hello, it's so nice to see you again!" said Barky politely.

One of the four birds looked at him strangely. Barky felt a little awkward. He soon realized why the other bird was staring at him. He was soaked all the way through! His feathers had flopped as if he had been swimming in the lake for a whole day.

Embarrassed, he shook slightly to rid himself of some of the water. The movement caused the power line to sway back and forth, back and forth, sending the blackbirds off balance. Darky and Larky flew off the power line and back in place between two other birds. They, too, were wet. Now many birds were flying up and down like a see-saw, chirping noisily.

"Chirpy! Chirpy! Chirp! Chirp!" They echoed each other loudly. As they chirped, they seemed to be saying:

It's exciting flying in the rain,

And it's exciting walking on the lawn.

Now, it's exciting sitting on the power lines,

Chirping silly jokes at each other!

Meanwhile, the other birds could not understand why the three little blackbirds were having so much fun but liked the sound of what Barky, Darky, and Larky were chirping. They joined in the chorus.

"Chirpy! Chirpy! Chirp! Chirp!"

"Chirpy! Chirpy! Chirp! Chirp!"

Soon, all the other blackbirds joined in the chorus. The sounds of "CHIRPY, CHIRPY, CHIRP, CHIRP" could be heard by everyone who stopped at the traffic light on that bleak afternoon. Some folks stared at the birds for a long time. Others pointed as they drove by. It was a spectacular moment!

Barky, Darky, and Larky felt proud of themselves. They were having fun and enjoying the melodious chorus of bird sounds ringing out around them:

"Chirpy! Chirpy! Chirp! Chirp!

Chirpy! Chirpy! Chirp! Chirp!

Chirpy! Chirpy! Chirp! Chirp!"

Hundreds of birds had joined in the parade. The chirping could be heard for miles along where the power lines extended, from North Street to South Street, and from East Street to West Street. As far as anyone could see, hundreds of blackbirds were sitting on the power lines. Every now and then, a few flew off only to settle back in position. Barky, Darky, and Larky had a lot of fun that late evening.

That night, the three little blackbirds cuddled into a hole in the big oak tree. This was an ideal place for their home while they stayed in the south. They were so tired that they soon fell asleep.

Barky, Darky, and Larky woke at dawn. They flew down from the big oak tree unto the lawn below. The morning dew on the grass was very enticing. As they walked around, they sang happily.

"CHIRPY! CHIRPY! CHIRP! CHIRP!

CHIRPY! CHIRPY! CHIRP! CHIRP!"

What a beautiful sight! Three little blackbirds walking on the lawn.

Printed in the United States
By Bookmasters